I0620981

Prove
All
Things

by
Betty Miller

First Edition Published 1980
Second Printing 1982
Third Printing 1983
Fourth Printing 1984
Fifth Printing 1987
Sixth Printing 1988
Seventh Printing 1989
Eighth Printing 1994
Ninth Printing 2001
Tenth Printing 2003
Print On Demand

Prove All Things

Copyright © 1980-2013

ISBN 1-57149-000-0

CHRIST UNLIMITED MINISTRIES, INC.
Pastor R.S. "Bud" Miller - Publisher
P.O. Box 850
Dewey, Arizona 86327
All Rights Reserved

Printed in U.S.A.

Scripture quotations are taken from the King James Version
unless otherwise indicated.

Contents

Preface

Greetings in the name of our Lord Jesus Christ:

I present this book to the body of Christ as the Holy Spirit presented it to me. I challenge you to allow God's Spirit of truth, and the Bible, to test the accuracy of the words within these pages. This book, part of the Overcoming Life Series, is also addressed to all seekers of truth who know not THE CHRIST UNLIMITED, as it would be my privilege to introduce you to Him.

During the early years of the ministry, I struggled to learn how to hear the voice of God. Once, while nervously waiting to speak before a large audience, and not being sure on what subject I should speak, I posed to the Lord in prayer this question: "Lord, what am I going to say to all these people?" In my spirit, I heard Him very clearly reply, "Betty, I was hoping you would not say anything, as I really wanted to speak." Yes, He wants to speak through us, as we yield to His Spirit. Submitting to the Lord and the guidance of the Holy Spirit, I found, was not only possible, but the only way He wants us to minister. **For it is not ye that speak, but the Spirit of your Father which speaketh in you (Matthew 10:20).**

This book is a gift from the Holy Spirit. I take no credit for it. If something within these pages blesses you, enlightens you, brings you closer to the Lord, releases you from fear or bondage, or heals or delivers you, then please lift your voice in praise to the precious Savior of our souls, Jesus Christ our Lord! On the other hand, if you find some of these things difficult to receive, hard to understand, or totally heretical from your viewpoint, would you also look to the Lord and ask Him if it could possibly be the truth? With an open and honest heart, will you ask God to change any pre-conceived ideas, and be free from traditions to receive of Him, His truth? His truth always brings freedom, never bondage. **And ye shall know the truth, and the truth shall make you free (John 8:32).**

In walking with the Lord, I have found we must obey the things we feel He is speaking to us. In my personal life, I used to be fearful of speaking for the Lord because I was so afraid of missing Him and making mistakes. (He, of course, has now delivered me of all my fears. Praise Him!) He encouraged me not to quit because of mistakes when He spoke these words to me: "Betty, if I receive the glory and praise for all the things that are a blessing to people, I also receive the responsibility for your mistakes, as long as you are striving to please me. I am able to make even those work for your good." **And we know that all things work together for good to them that love God, to them who are the called according to his purpose (Romans 8:28).** We serve a wonderful, loving God, who encourages us to follow and obey Him that we might be blessed, and in turn bless others!

This book was written as an act of obedience to the Lord, whom I dearly love. I consider it an honor to write for Him. Years ago, when I was in prayer, the Lord spoke that I was to write a book, but I never felt it was God's timing, nor did I feel the unction or anointing to begin this work until now. Over the past year God has performed a series of miracles to confirm that it is now His time, and has made the arrangements for this to become a reality.

I pray that this book, along with the Overcoming Life Series, may help you learn to walk closer to our Lord, as He is THE CHRIST UNLIMITED!

I am, by His love,
A handmaiden of the Lord,

Betty Miller
February, 1980

If any man will do his will, he shall know of the doctrine, whether it be of God, or whether I speak of myself (John 7:17).

Foreword

It just seemed natural that I would do the foreword on this book since my wife, Betty, and myself, are "one flesh." God, through the Holy Spirit, has given by revelation to Betty many truths of His Word, which have been set forth in this book.

The Lord spoke to Betty about ten years ago that she was to write a book for Him, and that He would arrange the right time and place to write it. Betty simply took this vision and set it aside until God began to "quicken" her spirit to bring it forth. One morning, very early, Betty awakened, and began to write as the Lord dictated to her. In giving her this small initial portion of the book, He showed her how, by submitting to His Spirit, and completely yielding to Him, He would feed to her the message He wanted to share with the body of Christ. He also revealed how quickly and easily it would be completed. The messages that God has given in this Overcoming Life Series are to all who desire to become "overcomers" and be "conformed to the image of His son" (**Romans 8:29**). Our Lord is not satisfied that a person remains a "babe" in Christ, but longs for each "babe" to grow to maturity. He desires that we should strive to become overcomers, live the overcoming life, and claim the promises of the inheritance of all things that are to be given to the overcomers.

I thank God that He has allowed me to share such close love and companionship with Betty. I know that within her heart she has no personal ambitions, no personal ends to achieve. Betty has simply been doing the will of the Father in the writing of this anointed book. May the Lord bless you with this book, as He has blessed us in being a part of His work.

Yours in Christ,

Pastor R.S. "Bud" Miller

He that overcometh shall inherit all things; and I will be his God and he shall be my son (Revelation 21:7).

Credits & Acknowledgments

ALL PRAISE AND CREDIT
GOES TO **THE CHRIST UNLIMITED!**

Truly Christ, the Father, and the Holy Spirit are to be praised, not only for this book, but for our very lives. His sacrifice on Calvary made it possible to know Him and all the members of God's family.

As with the printing of any book, there are lots of people responsible for the words on these pages, physical words as well as spiritual words. All the people that have ever been a part of my life, all the people that have prayed and supported this ministry, my friends and my family have truly contributed to this work. Special credit should be given to my husband, Bud, whose faithful and loving prayers, encouragement, leadership, and love are a big part of this book. Also, to everyone whose books and articles I've read, to the ministers of the Gospel, whose sermons I've heard, I express my gratitude. For each has contributed, in some measure, to this book. The list is endless, but eternity has the records. So instead of naming individuals on this page and giving them earthly credit, I prefer the Lord Jesus Christ to reward them each as only He can. God bless you all, and may you be surprised as you open up the box that contains your heavenly treasures.

For the Son of man shall come in the glory of his Father with his angels; and then he shall reward every man according to his works (Matthew 16:27).

Introduction

PROVE ALL THINGS is a guideline for "proving" the things that are of God and the things that are false. Christ warned that great deception would be one of the signs of the end times. In this book, instruction is given on how to recognize false prophets and teachings. Clear Scriptural guidelines are given on discerning the Spirit of truth versus the spirit of error. The book deals with how to judge without being judgmental.

We must be balanced in our approach to receiving new things to make sure they are from God. We can be so open we can allow the lies of Satan to deceive us. Yet on the other hand we can be closed minded because of fear and miss new truths of God. This book presents the Biblical standard for testing spiritual experiences to see which voice we are hearing. A major trick of the enemy is to get Christians to receive something they think is from God that will ultimately destroy them. We need to be aware of these devices without being fearful of receiving the wrong things.

PROVE ALL THINGS covers more than just discerning wrong doctrine; it also explains the way to test spiritual experiences as to their origin. How can we know if certain men and women are speaking God's truths? Prayerfully, this book will help you to determine the truth from error and follow the Master's voice.

Prove All Things

I Thessalonians 5:21: Prove all things; hold fast that which is good.

Recognizing False Prophets

One does not arrive at being an overcomer until he first learns the all important lesson of testing or "proving" the issues of this life. In the hour that we live, there are so many things that are false and evil. We must be constantly on guard and "prove" or test things, lest we become ensnared by something that is wicked. Cults are spreading. Eastern idolatrous religions are creeping into our country in very subtle forms, and many Christians are being deceived and have accepted their practices without even being aware of their evil. Some religious groups have existed for years under the guise of Christianity, and yet are far from the teachings of Jesus Christ. The Lord warns us of these false teachers and tells us to beware of them.

Looking at **Matthew 7:15-23**, we find Jesus gives us the guideline for determining false prophets:

Beware of false prophets, which come to you in sheep's clothing, but inwardly they are ravening wolves. Ye shall know them by their fruits. Do men gather grapes of thorns, or figs of thistles? Even so every good tree bringeth forth good fruit; but a corrupt tree bringeth forth evil fruit. A good tree cannot bring forth evil fruit, neither can a corrupt tree bring forth good fruit. Every tree that bringeth not forth good fruit is hewn down, and cast into the fire. Wherefore by their fruits ye shall know them. Not every one that saith unto me, Lord, Lord, shall enter into the kingdom of heaven; but he that doeth the will of my Father which is in heaven. Many will say to me in that day, Lord, Lord, have we not prophesied in thy

1

name? and in thy name have cast out devils? and in thy name done many wonderful works? And then will I profess unto them, I never knew you: depart from me, ye that work iniquity.

Certainly, we are admonished to be on guard. However, some go to such extremes as to become narrow-minded and closed to some beautiful truths in the name of being careful. What should our role as Christians be in regard to acceptance of a new thought, idea or doctrine? We are told to prove all things, not to reject them because they might be strange or new to us. However, we should not receive them either, until we first prove them. How do we prove things? All true Christians are in agreement that our standard is the Word of God, the Bible. God left us this Book as a reference, standard, or gauge so we could know whether something is good or evil, truth or error, right or wrong. (**2 Timothy 3:16-17: All scripture is given by inspiration of God, and is profitable for doctrine, for reproof, for correction, for instruction in righteousness: That the man of God may be perfect, thoroughly furnished unto all good works.**)

One of our major faults as Christians is that we tend to quote men on certain subjects instead of referring to the Book God gave us. We recognize that God gave us men to lead us into the truths of God, but our problem becomes who are the true men of God and who are the false ones that Christ warned us about? Sometimes we tend to evaluate men according to the size of their ministries, their popularity with men, or their endowment of certain gifts, etc.

The Lord said in verse **20 of Matthew 7** that we would know them by their fruits. What are these fruits? **Galatians 5:22-24** defines them as being the fruit of the Spirit. **But the fruit of the Spirit is love, joy, peace, longsuffering, gentleness, goodness, faith, meekness, temperance: against such there is no law. And they that are Christ's have crucified the flesh with the affections and lusts.** We are told to look at their lives and see if these fruits are predominant in them and examine if they are living

2

the crucified life. Of course, we must allow for imperfections that have not been overcome yet; but we should readily see the fruit of the Spirit in more abundance than the imperfections. One way we can check this is to notice the words that a man speaks. The Scripture says in **Matthew 12:33-35, Either make the tree good, and his fruit good; or else make the tree corrupt, and his fruit corrupt: for the tree is known by his fruit. O generation of vipers, how can ye, being evil, speak good things? for out of the abundance of the heart the mouth speaketh. A good man out of the good treasure of the heart bringeth forth good things: and an evil man out of the evil treasure bringeth forth evil things.**

Many people have been led astray when they could have recognized the wrong spirit simply by the braggadocios and prideful words of men who exalted themselves instead of Christ. Others would have been spared if they had examined the lifestyles of certain men who claim to be God's anointed if their lifestyles are far from being temperate; reflecting the most expensive and extravagant clothes, diamonds, homes, cars, etc. This is not referring to well-dressed men and women, and nice homes, but the extremes which reveal anything but the nature of Christ. Of course, neither is the other extreme of poverty the nature of Christ. Men of God should live temperate, moderate lives, overcoming poverty and avoiding extreme wealth. Jesus always went about giving to the poor. He never stored up His wealth even though He apparently handled a lot of money, thus the need for a treasurer, Judas. He gave away the things He could have used on Himself, yet He never lacked as He went about ministering. He should be our example today. The affection and lust for the things of this world do not portray the Spirit of Christ.

Examining the conversation of these leaders can quickly reveal the God they serve. Do they speak of God's kingdom, His righteousness, and His love; or does their conversation center on the things of this world and life? Are they peacemakers, sowing mercy and love? Are they gentle and patient, or do they lose their temper easily? Do they walk in faith, or are they continually looking to other men for their needs to be supplied? Are they always pressuring people for money, or do they simply receive those gifts of money as unto the Lord? Do they have the joy of the Lord, or do they minister out of duty? Are they truly joyous with that joy spilling over to others, or do they continually complain and gripe over all the things that are not pleasing to them? Is goodness evident in their lives instead of evil? Do they put people in bondage by always threatening them with the wrath of God, or is freedom of choice extended with the warning of the penalties of sin? Jesus came to set us free, not to bring us under the bondage of men.

Let us prove all leaders and see if their fruit is good fruit. Do they love and not hate, have joy instead of depression, and promote peace instead of strife? Are they longsuffering (patient) or impatient, gentle or harsh? Do they walk in faith, or doubt and unbelief? Are they meek, giving God the glory for their talents and gifts? Or do they pridefully talk of all they are doing or their group is doing? Does temperance prevail not only in their lifestyle, but in their personal habits as well? Or do extremes exist that do not glorify God? In essence they will not live for themselves, but for others as Jesus did. They will live a crucified life that glorifies God!

Proverbs 20:11 says, **Even a child is known by his doings, whether his work be pure, and whether it be right.**

Examining lives by this standard we must be careful not to go to extremes ourselves and expect total perfection of all ministers. There are many godly men and women who are called of God, who have overcome in many areas, although they still have some weak areas. They are believing as they walk with the Lord that these too will be perfected.

Proving Counsel

God's people sometimes have a tendency to exalt a pastor or teacher to a position that he or she certainly doesn't covet. God's

4

leaders were set in the body of Christ to help lead or bring us to Christ, not act as Christ for us. **Ephesians 4:11-15** says:

And he gave some, apostles; and some, prophets; and some, evangelists; and some, pastors and teachers; For the perfecting of the saints, for the work of the ministry, for the edifying of the body of Christ: Till we all come in the unity of the faith, and of the knowledge of the Son of God, unto a perfect man, unto the measure of the stature of the fullness of Christ: That we henceforth be no more children, tossed to and fro, and carried about with every wind of doctrine, by the sleight of men, and cunning craftiness, whereby they lie in wait to deceive; But speaking the truth in love, may grow up into him in all things, which is the head, even Christ.

God's men and women will help others to come into that place where they are perfected or mature. People sometimes want ministers to do all their praying and Bible study for them instead of taking the responsibility to do it themselves. Then, when that minister fails or gets into error, the person who has not studied or prayed for himself falls into the same lie with him. If they had been following the Lord, instead of a man, they would not have fallen into this trap. Instead they would have discerned the error and prayed for that man of God, so that he too might have seen the light and been corrected. The prayers of the people could have altered the minister's course.

People sometimes even want their ministers to make decisions for them. It is so much easier than seeking God for their answers and looking to His word. God's true ministers will not take the position that God should have in our lives. They will pray with us, but will not act as a substitute for our own personal prayer life. They will advise us, but never tell us we must choose a certain course. The true minister will present what God's Word says on a subject and the consequences we incur if we break God's laws and His Word, but he will always leave the individuals to make their own choices; never will he dominate, threaten, or coerce people to do certain things. The true man of God will pray

5

and allow the Holy Spirit to do the convincing, wooing, and leading of the individual.

On our end, we should prove the counsel the minister gives us. We should check it with God's Word, spend time in prayer, and see if it bears witness with our spirits. Taking our problems to our pastor, we should never elevate a minister's advice and word to being equal with God's Word, unless that word lines up with the Word of God. Prophecies should also be examined in the light of the Holy Spirit and God's Word. God's true ministers are servants and they never dominate another's life but always extend freedom. Even when the counsel given is God's, should the person refuse to listen, the true man of God allows the person freedom to make a mistake while surrounding him with much prayer, love, and mercy.

Guarding the Ear-Gate

In **Mark 4:24** the Lord warns us to **Take heed what ye hear.** The sound Scriptural basis for examining the things we hear teachers or pastors say is found in this verse. There are many godly shepherds who love their flocks, yet the Lord knew there would be those that would come in sheep's clothing, so He admonished us to "watch." A pastor who tells his flock that he alone has full revelation from God is, at best, vain and narrow- minded, and at worst, satanic. Such a shepherd is putting himself in the position of God. In effect, he is saying that God speaks only through him.

The Holy Spirit does not force, coerce, intimidate, or use fear to direct us. He always gives us choice and freedom. Anything that brings bondage is not of the Lord, and neither is anything that involves domination of another. It is the enemy, Satan, working through people that will cause them to dictate to others because it gives them the feeling of power. They want to control the lives and thinking of everyone with whom they deal.

Some people submit to this sort of doctrine because they

refuse to take responsibility for making their own decisions. God does not intend for people to evade responsibilities for their lives and their actions. God intends for us to grow spiritually throughout our lifetime. There is no possibility of growth if we don't make decisions and live with the consequences of those decisions. Certain people want to roll blithely through life absolved of all responsibility. Those with weak wills fall prey to the enemy coming through false prophets. We are warned to beware.

Spirit of Truth Vs. Spirit of Error

Should we disagree with a minister or a portion of his teaching, we shouldn't immediately call him a false prophet, but seek the Lord as to what is truth and what is error. He could have 95% truth and 5% error and still be a man of God. We shouldn't label people false simply because we disagree, but should seek the Lord as to what is truth. Yet, on the other hand, we shouldn't accept everything we hear as being the truth just because we admire or respect a man or woman. **I John 4:1-8** gives us a guideline as to how to test or prove the spirits:

Beloved, believe not every spirit, but try the spirits whether they are of God: because many false prophets are gone out into the world. Hereby know ye the Spirit of God: Every spirit that confesseth that Jesus Christ is come in the flesh is of God: And every spirit that confesseth not that Jesus Christ is come in the flesh is not of God: and this is that spirit of antichrist, whereof ye have heard that it should come; and even now already is it in the world. Ye are of God, little children, and have overcome them: because greater is He that is in you, than he that is in the world. They are of the world: therefore speak they of the world, and the world heareth them. We are of God: he that knoweth God heareth us; he that is not of God heareth not us. Hereby know we the spirit of truth, and the spirit of error. Beloved let us love one another: for love is of God; and every one that loveth is born of God, and

knoweth God. He that loveth not knoweth not God; for God is love.

The Lord tells us through John that anyone confessing that **Jesus Christ is come in the flesh** is of the Lord. This obviously doesn't mean that simply because a person is able to speak those words that he must be free of any false spirit. This has a much deeper meaning. Any religious doctrine that denies that Jesus came in the flesh is false. Those doctrines that deny that Jesus was born of a virgin are false and are ruled by the spirit of antichrist. Those groups who deny that Jesus is bodily coming again in the flesh are false. If they say, "He has already come, He came in the spirit," they are false because He is coming again in a physical body of flesh. The Word of God says He will come again in like manner as He left. (**Acts 1:11** says, **Which also said, Ye men of Galilee, why stand ye gazing up into heaven? this same Jesus, which is taken up from you into heaven, shall so come in like manner as ye have seen him go into heaven.**)

Those that deny His humanity, stressing only His deity, teach a false doctrine also. Jesus was totally man as well as totally God. The natural mind cannot comprehend this, but with the Holy Spirit we can understand and believe this. **I Timothy 2:5** says, **For there is one God, and one mediator between God and men, the man Christ Jesus,** while **John 14:10** says this, **Believest thou not that I am in the Father, and the Father in me? the words that I speak unto you I speak not of myself: but the Father that dwelleth in me, he doeth the works.** Every true doctrine will declare Christ's divinity as well as his humanity.

The other true doctrine that involves Jesus coming in the flesh is the fact that those who now believe in Christ and are "born again" have the Lord dwelling within their flesh. We can be baptized and filled with the Holy Spirit and have Jesus within us because of what He did on Calvary for us. We simply come to Him believing, repenting and asking Him to come and dwell in our hearts, and He performs that glorious miracle of the "new birth." The "new birth" which took place in Mary's womb when she conceived of the holy child Jesus can now be repeated. Instead of coming in the physical, in the womb, He comes spiritually in our hearts and we experience a "new birth." Old things are passed away and all things are made new. What a miracle that the God of the universe has chosen to come and dwell in us. The victory that Jesus obtained over death and the grave has made available to us the power of the Holy Spirit. We can live filled with that power every day!

The Spirit of Antichrist

The verses we are looking at in **I John 4** speak of the spirit of antichrist that is in false prophets. We know that "anti" means "against" and the Greek word for "Christ" is "The Anointed One." So this Scripture is telling us that anything that is against His anointing is the spirit of antichrist. What is His anointing? In the Old Testament the prophets used oil to anoint those who were called of God. Today we who are called by His name have His anointing within us. **1 John 2:27** says, **But the anointing which ye have received of him abideth in you...** The anointing is symbolized by the oil, and the oil represents the Holy Spirit. From this we can see that anything that opposes the Holy Spirit is "antichrist."

The Holy Spirit is represented always with power. We can now see that those who oppose the power of God are against Him. The Holy Spirit was given at Pentecost to give the disciples power to witness. The gifts of the Holy Spirit are powerful gifts. (**1 Corinthians 12:8-10** says, **For to one is given by the Spirit the word of wisdom; to another the word of knowledge by the same Spirit; To another faith by the same Spirit; to another the gifts of healing by the same Spirit; To another the working of miracles; to another prophecy; to another discerning of spirits; to another divers kinds of tongues; to another the interpretation of tongues.**) These gifts are for power to speak words of God, power to heal, power to work miracles, power to speak in other tongues, power to discern spirits, etc.

9

Those that oppose the power of the Holy Spirit are really being influenced by the spirit of antichrist. Therefore we can see that any doctrine that opposes the power and gifts of the Holy Spirit is the spirit of error and not God's truth.

Continuing our teaching on discerning false doctrines taught by those who are in error, we are warned that this spirit exists, but we are not to be fearful of it because **1 John 4:4** tells us that **greater is He that is in you, than he that is in the world.** Since Jesus dwells in us and Satan is the god of this world, this means that through the Lord we have overcome the spirit of antichrist, the lies of the false prophets, and the works of the devil. (This of course only applies if we are committed to God and His will; if we are not, we are open for error to deceive us.) Notice too in this verse that John addresses them as little children. There is a lesson here of which we need to be aware. In testing or proving others' doctrines we should do so with a spirit of humility. We should come before the Lord as a little child, not with a "know-it-all" attitude. We should prayerfully ask God, "Am I wrong?" or "Lord, is this doctrine false and not of you?" Without humility on our part, we can be deceived also.

The Lord sums this lesson up on trying the spirits with two important ways by which we can know whether it is the spirit of truth or the spirit of error. He says that people that are in the world (remember the world system is ruled by Satan) will speak of the world, and those that are worldly minded will hear them. If we are truly dedicated to God we will not be interested in the things of this world, but our conversation will be on things above. (**Philippians 3:18-20** verifies this, **For many walk, of whom I have told you often, and now tell you even weeping, that they are the enemies of the cross of Christ: Whose end is destruction, whose God is their belly, and whose glory is in their shame, who mind earthly things. For our conversation is in heaven; from whence also we look for the Saviour, the Lord Jesus Christ.**) Notice also in **1 John 4:6** that those who are God's own will agree with one another, but those that are not God's, will not. The true people of God will bear witness to truth when they hear it. We may not always understand everything we hear (just as we don't understand everything in the Bible), but in our spirits we will witness that it is true. We have all had the experience of hearing a sermon and while agreeing with the preacher, suddenly we hear a statement to which we do not agree. The problem here is that one of us is in error, or we would agree or witness with his or her statement. There is a possibility that it is on our end that the error exists. We need to humbly submit the thing in question to the Lord and ask Him to show us if we are wrong, or if it is the preacher or teacher. We need to go to the Word of God and seek the answer in the Bible. We should not take another's word unless it agrees with God's Word. If truth is being spoken through someone, we who have the Spirit of Truth within us will be able to witness to and hear that truth.

Another test we can apply is pointed out in **verse 8 of 1 John 4**. What kind of spirit is behind the things being said? Is it the spirit of love? The Scripture says, **He that loveth not knoweth not God; for God is Love.** A spirit that is pushy, arrogant, overbearing, rude, impatient, argumentative, envious, touchy, or prideful is not the spirit of love (**1 Corinthians 13**). Even when the spirit of God ministers a strong word it will have God's authority, stability, and love undergirding it. We are to try (test) the spirits and not receive everything we hear, yet we are to always have this balanced with a teachable spirit so that the Holy Spirit can correct us when necessary.

Prove All Things

Not only are we to test or try the spirits in men, but we are to do the same with any supernatural manifestations that we might experience. Today, when the world is being exposed to so many false things we need to be careful not to expose our spirits to false dreams, visions, revelations, prophecies, voices, etc. The Word of God definitely teaches that God can manifest Himself in any, or

11

all, of the above things; yet we are not to accept everything that comes in the name of Jesus. We need to test or prove these also. One of Satan's greatest devices is to counterfeit the real things of God and come to us disguised as the working of the Holy Spirit.

How do we test these things? Let us look to God's Word, as there is always wisdom there to show us what is truth. **James 3:13-18** says:

Who is a wise man and endued with knowledge among you? let him shew out of a good conversation his works with meekness of wisdom. But if ye have bitter envying and strife in your hearts, glory not, and lie not against the truth. This wisdom descendeth not from above, but is earthly, sensual, devilish. For where envying and strife is, there is confusion and every evil work. But the wisdom that is from above is first pure, then peaceable, gentle, and easy to be intreated, full of mercy and good fruits, without partiality, and without hypocrisy. And the fruit of righteousness is sown in peace of them that make peace.

From this Scripture we can know that anything that causes confusion, strife, or envy is of the devil.

Many times a dream will bring confusion, and by this we can know that it is not of God. If a prophecy is given to us and it causes fear or strife within us, we can know it is not of God. Some would say maybe it is a dream with a warning. God's warnings will always leave a way out for us; never will He leave us in hopelessness or despair. Satan has stepped up his work at this last hour and is sending many false spirits to cause many false spiritual manifestations to occur. This can especially happen to anyone who has ever been involved with the occult. If we receive devilish wisdom, we will find it will create not only strife, fear and confusion, but also every evil work. The evil lies which Satan tells people that lead them to destroy their lives and marriages are spawned in the pit of hell. He tells people lies such as the following: God has another mate for them that is more spiritual than the one they have; their mate is standing in the way of God blessing them, so they should leave; or, God has a soul mate for them, and now that they are following God they should have the mate God has chosen for them, etc. All of these are lies and can be exposed as we look at this Scripture.

God's wisdom is first pure, then peaceable. We are to be peacemakers, not involving ourselves in the war of divorce. We are to have pure hearts toward our mates and family, even if those mates or loved ones are not walking in the light we have, or even if they refuse to walk in it. We are to overcome evil with good. **Romans 12:21** states, **Be not overcome of evil, but overcome evil with good.** Our prayers, our love and our obedience to Christ will bring the victory in the lives of those that are the closest to us, as we follow in God's ways. Any revelation that does not encompass God's love is not of Him.

Is the voice we heard gentle? Or is it urgent and demanding? God is generally not in a big hurry. One of His virtues is patience. Usually, a demanding voice is not the Lord. Our Lord is gentle and kind.

Is our vision easy to be entreated? Or is it hard to believe? If it is difficult for us to receive, or beyond our imagination, we should examine it as to whether it came from the Lord or not. God's words are easy to be entreated.

Is our prophecy or vision full of mercy? Or is it instead harsh, threatening the wrath of God upon us or someone else? God is a God of love and He does not send tragedy, curses, sickness or fear upon His own children. If we have a dream or vision with such as this happening, it is not from our Lord. It is the devil trying to torment us and fill us with fear. If we are living for the Lord, the devil has no right to put his curse on us. If we are living for the devil, then we need to repent and get our lives right with God. Then we will not have to fear what Satan would try to do to us, for we have been given the power to overcome him (**Luke 10:19**). Sometimes people do have a dream of Satan's plan to destroy someone. If this should happen, we can pray and offset any of the enemy's plans. Some people may have a "feeling" that something bad will happen, and then it does. They call it a hunch or a pre-monition. When another premonition occurs they live in fear because of their initial experience; in their mind they believe it will happen again. Due to their belief it usually does come to pass. As Christians, our belief and trust should be in God, not our "feelings."

Bad dreams and feelings can be averted through the power of the Holy Spirit. As Christians, we do not have premonitions, but we receive a burden in the spirit for someone or something. This prayer burden is given to us to offset the plans of the enemy. As we stop and pray, we can overcome whatever he has planned. We can stay one step ahead of the enemy with the Lord on our side. It is truly wonderful to walk with Christ and be aware of the devices of Satan and defeat him first -- before he comes against us. **(Psalm 21:8**: **Thine hand shall find out all thine enemies: thy right hand shall find out those that hate thee.)**

We discussed the fruit of the Holy Spirit as being evident in our lives when we are walking with the Lord. **James 3:17** also mentions fruits. Does our dream, revelation or vision produce good fruit (love, joy, peace, longsuffering, gentleness, goodness, faith, meekness, and temperance)?

James continues and tells us that wisdom from above is without partiality and without hypocrisy. Many people get in trouble with false revelation because they think they are the only ones that are receiving a vision. They believe they are "special" unto God, or that God has a "special work" for them that no one else could do. God is not a partial God; He will use anyone who obeys and follows Him. God always extends His hand to "whosoever will." **Revelation 22:17** says, **...And whosoever will, let him take the water of life freely.** Deceiving spirits can work on a man's or woman's pride and/or ego by telling them they are God's anointed and special servants, and that they are the only ones able to perform certain tasks. If they would stop and examine the hypocrisy of their walk with God, they would know that they are not hearing God's voice.

God's pattern is to call us "to be" before He calls us "to do."

14

So many "babes" in Christ are eager to zealously go forth in a full-time ministry to save the world, yet they are not prepared for this task. **Romans 10:2** says, **For I bear them record that they have a zeal of God, but not according to knowledge.** We must have the knowledge of God's Word, which takes some preparation time, before we can go forth as an effective tool of the Lord. The real ministry flows from what Christ is doing "in us," not from what we are trying "to do" for Christ. It is always a greater service that we render through our "being" than through our "doing." It is a greater honor to be called to "be" something than to "do" something. Faith and preparation should precede "works." A true ministry will be an overflow of our fellowship and relationship with Jesus Christ. It will just spill over on to others.

James ends **chapter 3** by saying that the fruit of righteousness is sown in peace of them that make peace. The Amplified Version of **James 3:18** really makes it clear how to know if a revelation is from the Lord or the enemy. We can know by looking at the fruit. **And the harvest of righteousness (of conformity to God's will in thought and deed) is (the fruit of the seed) sown in peace by those who work for and make peace -- in themselves and in others, (that is,) that peace which means concord (agreement, harmony) between individuals, with undisturbedness, in a peaceful mind free from fears and agitating passions and moral conflicts.** From this we can examine the voices we are hearing to be sure they are the Lord's, and not those of the enemy, as the Lord's dealings will always produce good fruit. We can then know if we are receiving true or false wisdom. Confusion always occurs when we are fighting a battle to determine truth versus error. We must go to God to determine truth. We must find out if our confusion is resulting from God trying to show us error or Satan trying to rob us of truth. If our hearts are right and we sincerely desire to know the truth, God will reveal it to us. We must not set a time limit on God as to when we shall receive the truth. Some truths come quickly, others we must seek for diligently with our whole heart. **Matthew 7:7** in the Amplified Version says, **Keep on asking and it will be given you; keep on seeking and you will find; keep on knocking (reverently) and the door will be opened to you.**

Some people have thought that if they have asked God to take their vision or revelation out of their hearts and it still remains there, that it must be God. This is not necessarily so, as they must have perfect faith, a cleansed heart, and the willingness to suffer loss of their vision. We cannot say one prayer and expect to have instant truth in all areas of our life. We grow in truth as we walk with the Lord. The more we study His Word and the more we fellowship with Him, the more truth we possess. If, or when we come to the place where we are filled with His truth and faith, then those things we ask will be granted; but this place in Christ is the place of the overcomer. If we were in that place, all that we would speak would come to pass, and we would walk in the same authority that Christ walked in while He was on this earth. We would not have to tell people we were overcomers, as it would be evident, just as it was in Jesus' life. **John 15:7** shows us that it is possible to come to that place as it says, **If ye abide in me, and my words abide in you, ye shall ask what ye will, and it shall be done unto you.** Most of us are striving to reach that place. So until we do, we must keep taking things to God to check and see if they are from Him.

We must give all our desires, dreams and visions to the Lord to be perfected and given back to us, as He sees fit. We usually experience the death of a vision or dream before it can be resurrected. We see this in the life of Joseph. He received a true vision, but He did not understand it nor know the time of its occurrence. God's thoughts, techniques, and timing are different from man's (**Isaiah 55:8-9**). We must realize when we are still young in the Lord, there is much cleansing of the carnal mind that must take place before our thoughts and our hearts are trustworthy. (**Jeremiah 17:9-10** says, **The heart is deceitful above all things, and desperately wicked: who can know it? I the Lord search**

16

the heart, I try the reins, even to give every man according to his ways, and according to the fruit of his doings.**)

A Vision of God or Satan

If we persist in our own way and our own vision, we could even receive it, but it would not be the highest and best for our lives. We could miss the life of an overcomer by demanding things in the flesh. If we truly desire to do the Lord's will, then we must be willing to be corrected and even embarrassed, if that's what it takes to set right the things that are wrong. Until the renewing of our carnal mind takes place, we need to continually check out all things with the Lord by prayer and His Word, so that we will not be deceived by the devil with a false dream or vision.

Even though Satan gives counterfeit visions, God gives true ones. One type of vision God gives is a "warning vision." The Lord will warn people if they are sinning and refuse to quit what will happen to them because of their disobedience. He does not plan tragedy as it comes only as a result of their sin and rebellion. The Lord desires for them to repent so that judgment may be averted. (**2 Chronicles 7:14** says, **If my people, which are called by my name, shall humble themselves, and pray, and seek my face, and turn from their wicked ways; then will I hear from heaven, and will forgive their sin, and will heal their land.**)

He also gives us visions for the future so that we can walk today with hope in Him. With our days filled with struggles, troubles, and the fight of faith, we need a vision in our hearts so we can press on in the Lord. **Proverbs 29:18** states, **Where there is no vision, the people perish...** We must have hope in our hearts to continue when things are difficult. Some things we cannot do today for the Lord, but God has those reserved for a future time when we are ready for those responsibilities in His kingdom. However, there are so many things we can do today. We can share the love that Christ has brought to us with those in our homes and communities.

Each of us has the ministry of reconciliation. **And all things are of God, who hath reconciled us to himself by Jesus Christ, and hath given to us the ministry of reconciliation; To wit, that God was in Christ, reconciling the world unto himself, not imputing their trespasses unto them; and hath committed unto us the word of reconciliation. Now then we are ambassadors for Christ, as though God did beseech you by us: we pray you in Christ's stead, be ye reconciled to God. (2 Corinthians 5:18-20**). From this verse we can see that each Christian, no matter how long he has walked with the Lord, has the ministry of reconciling others to God. God will give us the holy boldness to proclaim the gospel to others if we but ask Him for it. He desires to use each of us to win souls for Him. This is one ministry that young Christians excel in as they are eager to share with others what they have found in Christ. If we will be content to let God use us where we are, then He will prepare us to reach out unto the ends of the world. We read in **Acts 1:8**, Jesus' words, **But ye shall receive power, after that the Holy Ghost is come upon you: and ye shall be witnesses unto me both in Jerusalem, and in all Judea, and in Samaria, and unto the uttermost part of the earth.** If we are faithful to serve Him in our small worlds of home and office, He will expand our outreach to a worldwide ministry. **Matthew 25:23** states, **His lord said unto him, Well done, good and faithful servant; thou hast been faithful over a few things, I will make thee ruler over many things: enter thou into the joy of thy lord.** We need to allow God to use us where we are, and He will then increase our sphere of influence.

We need to test and prove our calling. Is God calling me to go now, or later? Many sell all and go, thinking to follow Christ, only to find they are not yet trained to handle the responsibilities of a ministry. One of the first things that usually happens is an attack by Satan that overwhelms them. Because they are not yet trained in spiritual warfare, they do not know how to get the victory. The Lord must train us to be strong warriors in the battle of prayer, so we can overcome the enemy every time. Even if we get ahead of the Lord, but our hearts are right with Him, He will correct our course so that we do not end as shipwrecked. However, sidetracks and disasters could be prevented if we sought the Lord diligently before we moved out in a ministry.

Usually there is a period of time between our "call" from God and the actual ministry becoming a reality. We see this in the disciples' lives as they were called by Jesus, then trained by Him before He sent them out two by two. Paul, after his conversion, went to Arabia for about three and one-half years before he came back to Jerusalem to begin ministering. Before we go forth, let us submit to God's cleansing and proving so that we will be able to stand and be an example to others, as they seek God's will for their lives.

One reason some people move too quickly to do the things they believe to be God is that they are fearful of disobeying Him, and thereby angering Him. They do not yet understand the loving and patient nature of our Father. The Lord never minds us testing or trying things to see if He is in them. It is only when we put God on trial that we do wrong. If we come to Him with a humble and sincere heart, wanting to know the answer to an honest question, He is more than willing to reveal to us the truth about the matter. The only time we will not get an answer from God is when we approach Him rebelliously, demanding an answer from Him.

When to Judge

Many Christians are hesitant about proving or testing things as they tend to categorize this right along with "judging," and they have been taught they are to judge no man. Most of us are familiar with the Scripture in **Matthew 7:1** that says, **Judge not, that ye be not judged.** If we look at only this one verse, and we are trying to judge a situation, we will feel guilty about making an evaluation. However, we should look at all the other Scriptures related to this one, so we know how we are to judge. Let us continue to read the rest of this Scripture, **For with what judgment ye judge, ye shall be judged: and with what measure ye mete, it shall be measured to you again. And why beholdest thou the mote that is in thy brother's eye, but considerest not the beam that is in thine own eye? Or how wilt thou say to thy brother, Let me pull out the mote out of thine eye; and, behold, a beam is in thine own eye? Thou hypocrite, first cast out the beam out of thine own eye; and then shalt thou see clearly to cast out the mote out of thy brother's eye (Matthew 7:2-5).**

Examining all these Scriptures, we see that Jesus is not saying we are not to judge, but rather how we are to judge.

Our judgment should be merciful. The judgment we judge others with will be the same way we shall be judged. Jesus had just instructed the people in His sermon on the mount, **Blessed are the merciful: for they shall obtain mercy (Matthew 5:7).** We can see here that we are able to "store up" mercy. If we want others to be merciful to us when we fail and make mistakes, we must extend mercy to those that we now see who are making mistakes.

1 Corinthians 6:1-8 also tells us we are to judge:

Dare any of you, having a matter against another, go to law before the unjust, and not before the saints? Do ye not know that the saints shall judge the world? and if the world shall be judged by you, are ye unworthy to judge the smallest matters? Know ye not that we shall judge angels? How much more things that pertain to this life? If then ye have judgments of things pertaining to this life, set them to judge who are least esteemed in the church. I speak to your shame. Is it so, that there is not a wise man among you? No, not one that shall be able to judge between his brethren? But brother goeth to law with brother, and that before the unbelievers. Now therefore there is utterly a fault among you, because ye go to law one with another. Why do ye not rather take wrong? Why

do ye not rather suffer yourselves to be defrauded? Nay, ye do wrong, and defraud, and that your brethren.

We are going to one day judge angels (the angels spoken about here are the fallen angels that were cast out of heaven down to earth and are now the evil spirits that roam the earth under Satan's dominion). If we are to do this, we must begin by making judgments on this earth.

We need to judge according to God's Word. We are to see if things line up with the Word of God. If we see sin in our own lives, or in others, we must call it sin. Then, we are to pray for those that are in sin, asking the Lord to deliver them. We are to ask counsel from those in the church that are wise and humble. We are not to go to those in the world.

Specifically, in these verses Paul is dealing with lawsuits between Christians. He says it is a shame for Christians to go to court against one another. He encourages Christians to give up their rights and suffer loss of worldly things so as not to bring reproach upon the church. We see this sadly lacking in Christians today as there are even cases of ministries suing their elders over ownership of church buildings when church splits occur. What a shame for Christ's body, fighting over material possess instead of going before God and giving Him everything, allowing Him to do our battling for us **(1 Samuel 17:47)**. He is able to defend us or restore to us our material losses, if we only allow Him to have control over situations that seem unfair. Our attitudes are so much more important to God than maintaining our "rights." Above all things, the Lord is interested in the love that is perfected in our hearts. **For all the law is fulfilled in one word, even in this; Thou shalt love thy neighbour as thyself. But if ye bite and devour one another, take heed that ye be not consumed one of another. (Galatians 5:14-15).** Fighting and going to court with Christians or non-Christians will only produce destruction for all parties. If we were walking in the Spirit, we would not get involved in the things of the flesh. **And if any man will sue** thee at the law, and take away thy coat, let him have thy cloke also (Matthew 5:40).

Scripturally, we see that we can judge. In **1 Corinthians 2:14-16** Paul writes, **But the natural man receiveth not the things of the Spirit of God: for they are foolishness unto him: neither can he know them, because they are spiritually discerned. But he that is spiritual judgeth all things, yet he himself is judged of no man. For who hath known the mind of the Lord, that he may instruct him? But we have the mind of Christ.** This states we must have the mind of Christ on matters to be able to make proper judgments. We are to have spiritual discernment and not make judgments in the flesh. It does not matter what we may think of a situation; the important thing is knowing the mind of the Lord. Man's carnal judgments are not "after the Spirit" because he cannot see into people's hearts. If we could see the inner man, we would not judge harshly those that are truly trying to overcome, but are weak and continue to fail. We would extend love and mercy. Jesus exemplified this in the account of the woman who was caught in the act of adultery. When the Pharisees brought Him the woman for judgment, He spoke these words, **He that is without sin among you, let him first cast a stone at her (John 8:7).** The punishment under the old Jewish law was death by stoning for those who committed adultery.

The only times Jesus was ever severe in His judgment were in cases where men were hypocritical. In **Matthew 23:23** we find the following warning, **Woe unto you, scribes and Pharisees, hypocrites! for ye pay tithe of mint and anise and cummin, and have omitted the weightier matters of the law, judgment, mercy, and faith: these ought ye to have done, and not to leave the other undone. Verse 33** says, **Ye serpents, ye generation of vipers, how can ye escape the damnation of hell?** The reason the Lord could make this judgment is because He would lay down His life for these men who were rejecting Him. Before we make judgments on others, we too need to be ready to lay our lives down for those souls. We can do this by prayer, fasting, suffering under their ungodly remarks, and believing for their souls. In this way our judgment will be pure, as we are not passing judgment without sorrow in our hearts for them. We are never to pass judgment as a retaliation.

The next thing we need to check when judging is to see if we are being hypocritical by pointing to others while we are unwilling to correct the things wrong in our own lives. Perhaps the sin we see in others is only minor (mote), while in our lives there is a major sin (the beam), which we are refusing to acknowledge (see **Matthew 7:3-5**). Let us first deal with our own sin, before we judge the sin in others. **For if we would judge ourselves, we should not be judged. But when we are judged, we are chastened of the Lord, that we should not be condemned with the world (1 Corinthians 11:31-32**). How do we judge ourselves? This only comes as we see ourselves as guilty sinners who need a Saviour; for without Him we could not attain holiness nor be righteous. We must judge our own lives according to the Word of God. We must look and see how we are living up to the Word. When we do this we must be careful not to become legalistic. (We should obey from the heart and not bind ourselves to the letter of the law.)

This does not mean we are free to break God's laws, but we are free from the bondage of the law. When we sin, we feel guilty; and guilt brings bondage. The law was not made for the purpose of saving or justifying. It was made to show us our need of cleansing and to point us to the great source of cleansing, Jesus Christ, our Lord. The Bible speaks of the law as a mirror to show us what kind of people we really are. **For if any be a hearer of the word, and not a doer, he is like unto a man beholding his natural face in a glass: For he beholdeth himself, and goeth his way, and straightway forgetteth what manner of man he was. But whoso looketh into the perfect law of liberty, and continueth therein, he being not a forgetful hearer, but a doer of the work, this man shall be blessed in his deed (James 1:23-25**). It is obvious that a mirror (the law) cannot remove a spot from the face. Its work is to reveal the spot and to point the dirty one to the sink for the actual cleansing. The law, in like manner, only condemns the sinner by giving him knowledge of his condition, and then pointing him to the cross for true cleansing. **For by grace are ye saved through faith; and that not of yourselves: it is the gift of God: Not of works, lest any man should boast (Ephesians 2:8-9)**. Paul further emphasizes this point in **Galatians 2:16, Knowing that a man is not justified by the works of the law, but by the faith of Jesus Christ, even we have believed in Jesus Christ, that we might be justified by the faith of Christ, and not by the works of the law: for by the works of the law shall no flesh by justified.**

Right here we need to consider one of the most fallacious propositions ever set forth relating to the law. Countless sincere Christians have accepted the idea that the Old Testament encompasses the dispensation of works, and that the New Testament provides for a dispensation of grace, and their separate events are unrelated. Under this misconception, people were saved by works in the Old Testament and by grace in the New Testament. This is simply not true. The Bible holds forth only one beautiful, perfect, plan for anybody to be saved, and that is by grace through faith. Heaven will not be divided between those who got there by works and those who got there by faith. Every single soul among the redeemed will be a sinner saved by grace through faith. Those who entered into salvation in the Old Testament trusted the merits of the blood of Jesus Christ, demonstrating their faith by bringing a lamb and slaying it. They looked forward, in faith, to the atoning death of Jesus. We look back in faith to the same cross and are saved in exactly the same way, by faith in what Christ did on the cross for us. All the redeemed host throughout eternity will sing the same song of deliverance, exalting the Lamb slain from the foundation of the world. Law and grace do not work in competition with each other, but in perfect coordination. The law points out sin, and grace saves from sin.

The law is the will of God, and grace is His undeserved favor and power to do the will of God. We do not obey the law in order to be saved, but because we are saved. Although we live in the dispensation of grace, and the Old Testament saints lived under the dispensation of the law, both are still valid today as Jesus said in **Matthew 5:17, Think not that I am come to destroy the law, or the prophets: I am not come to destroy, but to fulfil.** From this Scripture we can see that the law is still valid in the New Testament.

An Old Testament example of God's grace being available then is recorded in the life of David. In the eleventh and twelfth chapters of **2 Samuel**, we have the story of David committing adultery and murder. Nathan the prophet was sent by God to David to convict and correct David. When he realized the gravity of his sin, David immediately repented and confessed his sin. Since David's heart was right, God was merciful and extended grace to him. The penalty for his sin was death by stoning; however, since he quickly repented, his sin was put away by God, showing that grace was indeed operating in the Old Testament. **And David said unto Nathan, I have sinned against the Lord. And Nathan said unto David, The Lord also hath put away thy sin; thou shalt not die (2 Samuel 12:13**). We live by His mercy and grace. Grace is His undeserved favor and divine enablement, while mercy requires no punishment for our sins. He took the punishment for us, so we don't have to take it. Praise God! Mercy deals with the negative side of our sin, while grace is positive since we receive things we do not merit.

Judging Ourselves

In judging ourselves, we need to come to the Lord and ask for cleansing and forgiveness as often as needed. We need to confess our faults to Him and others. (**James 5:16: Confess your faults one to another, and pray one for another, that ye may be healed. 1 John 1:9: If we confess our sins, he is faithful and just to forgive us our sins, and to cleanse us from all**

unrighteousness.) In confessing to other members of the body of Christ, we should have the Lord's guidance as to whom we should reveal our sins. Some people are unable to receive a confession, and it can do more harm than good. This is especially true if that person is not walking in the same spiritual light that you are. It is enough to confess those particular sins to God. Let the Holy Spirit guide you in these areas, as there are Christians that do not have Christ's nature of mercy formed in them yet, and they could use the confession against you, instead of receiving it as unto the Lord. We should not confess to those that are outside Christ, as they do not understand God's love and forgiveness.

Looking again to **1 Corinthians 11:31-32**, we see that if we judge ourselves, we shall not be judged; and if we are judged we are chastised of the Lord. How does the Lord chasten us? Does He do mean things to us? Does He send sickness, tragedy, etc. to straighten us up? No, He does not; the Father chastens us by His Word. Let us look at **John 12:47-48**; **And if any man hear my words, and believe not, I judge him not: for I came not to judge the world, but to save the world. He that rejecteth me, and receiveth not my words, hath one that judgeth him: the word that I have spoken, the same shall judge him in the last day.** As Christians, when we do wrong we are immediately chastised by the Spirit of God convicting us. If we lie, we hear the Word of God in our spirit say, **Thou shalt not lie.** We feel guilty and experience the Holy Spirit's disapproval. If we immediately repent and make things right with God and man, then we are restored to fellowship with God. If we refuse to repent and choose to continue in our sin, we add sin to sin and end up with a broken relationship with the Lord. He cannot fellowship with those that are in sin. He is a holy God. As long as this breach exists, we are not right with God and it leaves the door open for Satan to attack us. Satan then has a right to come and put sickness on us, bring accusations, send evil tidings, create fear in our hearts, etc., because we are in his territory. Our own sins and backsliding bring the problems. Our Lord does not send them to teach us something. (**Jeremiah 2:19, Thine own wickedness shall correct thee, and thy backslidings shall reprove thee: know therefore and see that it is an evil thing and bitter, that thou hast forsaken the Lord thy God...**)

Learning From the Word

The Lord teaches us by His Word, or His Book, the same way teachers teach their children in school, by the book. The word "chastise" in the Greek usually denotes "to train children." It suggests the broad idea of education by correcting with words, reproving, admonishing and instructing. When we can grasp this, we can then know that God is not the author of evil, but it is our wrong decisions that produce evil and its consequences. If we are walking defeated Christian lives, it is not God's fault. He made a way for us to overcome by obeying His Word. When the trials of life overwhelm us and we are defeated, it is because we did not pass the test. In school, when a child fails a test, we do not blame the teacher, as the fault lies with the child who did not do his lessons and homework well. However, when Christians fail the tests in life, may times it is God who is blamed. He gets the blame for taking little children's lives in accidents, for sending sickness upon His children, for burning down houses, for earthquakes, storms, etc. Could it be that if we did our homework by praying and studying the Bible, that many of these things could be prevented? Yes, they could; the lack is ours, not God's.

We believe in the motto, "Prayer Changes Things," yet how much quality time do we spend in prayer? How many hours do we devote to Bible study as compared to the hours we watch TV or devote our time to other time wasting endeavors? Yet, when something bad happens in our lives, we do not take the blame to ourselves because it is so much easier to blame God. God gave us mighty weapons in His Word to overcome the devil and defeat him at every turn. Is it His fault we are not aware of these weapons? We have the book that tells us how to be an overcomer. That book is the Holy Bible. I would say few people reading this would not have access to a Bible. The Holy Spirit is our teacher and His operation manual for living in this world is the Bible. If we have Him in our hearts and read His manual, there is not one problem that we cannot overcome. We find few overcomers because we find few apt students. We find a lot of people that know the Word of God but they do not apply it to their lives. In school we must apply what we know to pass the exams. If we do not know our subject, we are doomed to fail from the start. That is why we must know Him first, for in Him is all knowledge and wisdom.

If we are walking with the Lord, the Holy Spirit will always do His job of reproving us for sin. (**John 16:8**: **And when he (the Holy Spirit) is come, he will reprove the world of sin, and of righteousness, and of judgment....**) Sometimes we suffer under Satan's false accusations when we are not guilty at all. How can we determine when it is the Holy Spirit that is convicting us and when it is the enemy that is condemning us? When the Holy Spirit convicts us of sin, He always shows us the way out and always extends to us pardon. When the devil is condemning us, he never leaves us a way out, he accuses us, and he condemns us to failure. He would whisper to us, "You will never change; you can never overcome this weakness. God is angry with you and He will punish you for this. You might as well go back into the world. God's way is too hard. You are doomed to hell, anyway. Why, you have committed the unpardonable sin, etc." These are a few of the lies Satan tells us when we have failed and sinned, and every one of them brings condemnation and fear. God always lifts us up and helps us when we have failed Him, and shows us there is a better way. He enables us to overcome if we do it His way.

If we forsake evil and turn to Him, we are never condemned; but if we continue to sin, we are condemned along with the world. **John 3:18-21, He that believeth on him is not condemned: but he that believeth not is condemned already, because he hath not believed in the name of the only begotten Son of God. And this is the condemnation, that light is come into the** world, and men loved darkness rather than light, because their deeds were evil. For every one that doeth evil hateth the light, neither cometh to the light, lest his deeds should be reproved. But he that doeth truth cometh to the light, that his deeds may be made manifest, that they are wrought in God.** If we judge ourselves, we shall not be condemned with the world because we are a part of a "new world."

The Lord gave a parable in **Matthew 5:25-26** that gives us a guideline as to how we can judge ourselves and remain free from Satan's condemning lies. **Agree with thine adversary quickly, whiles thou art in the way with him; lest at any time the adversary deliver thee to the judge, and the judge deliver thee to the officer, and thou be cast into prison. Verily I say unto thee, Thou shalt by no means come out thence, till thou hast paid the uttermost farthing.** The Amplified Version of the Bible makes this even a little easier for us to understand. **Come to terms quickly with your accuser while you are on the way travelling with him, lest your accuser hand you over to the judge, and the judge to the guard, and you be put in prison; Truly, I say to you, you will never be released until you have paid the last fraction of a penny.** We know that Satan is our accuser and our adversary (**Revelation 12:10**), so when we are walking with him, or keeping company with him by sinning, and he accuses us of that sin, we are to agree with him. If we have lied, and he says to us, "You are a liar and all liars go to hell," we are to agree with this statement, when guilty. We must not stop here, however; we should then ask God's forgiveness and tell the devil, "Yes, I have sinned, but I have asked God to forgive me and His Word also says, **If we confess our sins, he is faithful and just to forgive us our sins, and to cleanse us from all unrighteousness (1 John 1:9**). If we do not confess our sin, then we come under the judge's jurisdiction. We find that the judge is the Word of God, and the Word of God does declare that all liars end up in hell. (**Revelation 21:8: But the fearful, and unbelieving, and the abominable, and murderers, and whoremongers, and sorcer-**

29

ers, and idolaters, and all liars, shall have their part in the lake which burneth with fire and brimstone: which is the second death.) So the judge (God's word) takes us to the officer or the guard. The guard is representative of the Holy Spirit, as He guards the Word. If the Holy Spirit does not know us, then we must pay the price for our sin.

By agreeing that we are guilty and asking the Lord for forgiveness, we can avoid the condemnation and the penalty. When Satan then accuses us, the Holy Spirit will have pardoned us because Jesus paid the price for our sins so that we do not have to pay it. Praise God! Even as Christians we can come into bondage and be held prisoner in our bodies, our emotions and our minds if we fail to ask for forgiveness of our sins. Satan has a legal hold when we have unconfessed sin in our lives. We should also ask the Lord to forgive us for those things that we do not, as of yet, recognize as sin, even as David did in **Psalm 19:12**: **Who can understand his errors? cleanse thou me from secret faults.** The more of God's Word that we know, the more we shall be able to recognize our sin and be cleansed of it. **Ephesians 5:26**: **That he might sanctify and cleanse it (the church) with the washing of water by the word...** Yes, the more of God's Word we have in our hearts, the more we shall be able to prove and test all things. To know and understand the Word of God is to know the truth, and in knowing the truth we indeed shall be free.

We then, being free, will not have to stand before God's judgment for sin. What is God's judgment on sin? It is the penalty for broken spiritual laws. This penalty is brought on by our own sins (unless we receive Jesus, as He took the penalty for us on Calvary). The judgment of God can be averted by repentance and prayer. Disasters come to cities, and most of the time it is spoken of as "the judgment of God" coming upon the people because of their wickedness. If Christians were praying for their cities and asking God to be merciful and to deliver and touch the people of that town, we would see fewer disasters. Christians should be in prayer daily for their communities, seeking God on behalf of the city officials and praying for truth and peace to reign in their local areas. We, as Christians, have been failing, thus allowing Satan to bring disaster to areas because there are no interceding Christians.

Sins of Omission

There are two kinds of sins. One is that of commission (sins that we commit) and the other of omission (things we omit). The sin of omission is the failure to do the things we know we should do. It is being committed every day when we fail to pray for our cities and governments (**James 4:17**). We might ask ourselves this question, "If it were up to us to be responsible in prayer for our city's welfare, would our prayers be sufficient for that task?" This will reveal to us that the lack is not on God's part, but on our part, in that we do not pray diligently. It will take more than a few times of praying, "God bless America," for our country to have a real revival and turn from its wickedness. It will take real intercessory prayer and spiritual warfare for the victory to be won.

God is not responsible for the tragedies in our homes, cities and country. We are responsible. **Ezekiel 22:30-32** says, **And I sought for a man among them, that should make up the hedge, and stand in the gap before me for the land, that I should not destroy it: but I found none. Therefore have I poured out mine indignation upon them; I have consumed them with the fire of my wrath: their own way have I recompensed upon their heads, saith the Lord God.** From this verse we can see that it is our evil ways that bring destruction, not God. Destruction is simply the result of sin. How terrible to blame God for tragedy and disaster! It is man's nature to do this, because it is much easier to blame God than to take responsibility for his own failures and sins. **Ezekiel 33:20** states, **Yet ye say, The way of the Lord is not equal. O ye house of Israel, I will judge you every one after his ways.** We see the Israelites were guilty of the same sin of blaming God for His alleged injustice, instead of see-

31

ing their own sins. They were God's people, yet they were full of sin. Today we find the same scene. Many of God's people are the very ones blaming God for their tragedies, losses of loved ones, sicknesses, sorrows, etc. They are blinded to their sin, as it has taken a subtle form of self-righteousness. They feel if they attend church regularly and give their tithes, they have fulfilled their obligations to God. They do not recognize their complacency and their love for the world, as many of the clergy have allowed them to bring the "world" into the church.

One of the greatest ills in the church today is the mixture of the church and the world. The church is no longer separated from the world, but looks just like the world. The world does not recognize Christians because they do the same thing the world does. They eat and drink the same things, go to the same places, etc. In **Exodus 12:38** we find an account of a people called the "mixed multitude."

The background of this account tells about Israel being led out of Egyptian bondage by Moses. When they left, some of the Egyptians who had married the Israelites left with them. Also there were those that were half-Egyptian and half-Israelite. The Old Testament has many accounts of "types" that are lessons for us today. **1 Corinthians 10:5-6** says, **But with many of them God was not well pleased: for they were overthrown in the wilderness. Now these things were our examples, to the intent we should not lust after evil things, as they also lusted.** The example we are to see here is a lesson of what happens to those who are not true Israelites at heart. We see in **Numbers 11** that after the Israelites had wandered in the wilderness awhile, they began to gripe and complain. This spirit spawned from those that were of the mixed multitude. The mixed multitude were those in the outermost part of the camp. They didn't come to the center of the camp where the tabernacle was pitched, as they didn't want to be exposed by the glory of the Lord. Their allegiance soon waned under trial and persecution, and they longed to go back to Egypt where the fish, cucumbers, melons, garlics, leeks, and onions were.

Soon their lust for these things overcame them, and they were destroyed by the fire of God and the wrath of the Lord.

Today we find the same problem in the church. The lust for the things of this world, plus uncommitted hearts that contain a mixture of this world and the Lord's kingdom, will ultimately bring the judgment of God. It was not God's intention for Israel to wander in the wilderness for 40 years, as He wanted to bring them to the promised land that was flowing with milk and honey. It is the same today; He wants to bless His children, but their rebellion and lack of commitment do not allow Him to do so. The Word of God proves we have a loving and just God. As we seek Him and grow in His Word, we will not suffer His judgment on sin. The judgment of the wrath of God comes only upon sin in this world. If we have Jesus in our hearts and have been forgiven of our sins and have renounced the things of this world, then we have no need to fear the wrathful judgment of God. It will not fall on God's children who are striving to follow Him. Praise God!

In concluding, let us look to God to prove all things. **Proving what is acceptable unto the Lord (Ephesians 5:10)**. Only by coming before Him with a teachable spirit can we be taught the truth and recognize error. As we become more acquainted with the real, we will be able to better discern the counterfeit. The devil has a counterfeit for every truth of God. However, we need not fear being deceived if we are in fellowship with the Lord, for He will deliver us from every evil as we continue to follow Him.

Our daily prayer should be "Lord, cleanse me from all error and renew my mind. Lord, I desire to know the truth even if it means correction and embarrassment for me. Change my thoughts and heart to be your thoughts."

Index

Revelations 11

S

Satan 6, 10, 12, 13, 14, 15, 17, 18, 21, 26, 28, 29, 30, 31

Sin 4, 17, 21, 22, 23, 24, 25, 26, 28, 29, 30, 31, 32

Supernatural 11

V

Visions 11, 16, 17

W

Wisdom 9, 12, 13, 14, 15, 28
Word of God 2, 6, 8, 11, 21, 23, 26, 28, 29, 30

Additional Books by the Author:

Book Titles in the OVERCOMING LIFE SERIES:

PROVE ALL THINGS
THE TRUE GOD
THE WILL OF GOD
KEYS TO THE KINGDOM
EXPOSING SATAN'S DEVICES
HEALING OF THE SPIRIT, SOUL & BODY
NEITHER MALE NOR FEMALE
EXTREMES OR BALANCE?
THE PATHWAY INTO THE OVERCOMER'S WALK

Book Titles in the END TIMES SERIES:

MARK OF GOD OR MARK OF THE BEAST
PERSONAL SPIRITUAL WARFARE

Christ Unlimited Ministries, Inc.
P.O. Box 850
Dewey, AZ 86327
U.S.A.
For online orders, please visit our website:
http://www.bibleresources.org

Postnote

The Millers are very glad to receive mail from their readers; however, they are unable to answer the letters personally due the volume of mail that they receive. They will be happy to pray along with their intercessors for all who write with a prayer request; although they do no outside counseling as they believe this should be directed to local pastors as outlined in Scripture.

Christ Unlimited Ministries, Inc. is a non-profit church 501(c) (3) corporation. All contributions are tax deductible. We appreciate your prayers, encouragement and support. Your purchase of this book makes it possible for us to share free copies of Bibles, teaching literature, tracts and downloadable audio/video materials with ministers in third world countries who would otherwise not be able to purchase them.

The Lord gave the word: great was the company of those that published it (Psalm 68:11).

For Additional Study

This book is taken from a course of Bible studies called the Overcoming Life Series. The entire series is a virtual "spiritual tool chest," as it covers a multitude of subjects every Christian faces in his walk with God. It also answers questions that many believers have concerning the current move of God. These are dealt with in a balanced approach and in the light of the Scripture. God's people are not to live frustrated, defeated lives, but rather they are to be victorious overcomers! Other books available with their companion workbooks are:

PROVE ALL THINGS - Christ warned that great deception would be one of the signs of the end times. In this book, instruction is given on how to recognize false prophets and teachings. Clear Scriptural guidelines are given on discerning the Spirit of truth versus the spirit of error. The book deals with how to judge without being judgmental.

THE TRUE GOD - This is a teaching on the character of God, explaining why God does certain things, and why it is against His nature to do other things. It differentiates between the things for which God is responsible and the things for which the devil is responsible. Our responsibility as Christians destined to overcome is made clear so that we can live victorious lives.

THE WILL OF GOD - This lesson teaches us not only how to know the will of God in our personal lives, family, ministry and finances, but also brings understanding as to why God allows sin, sickness and suffering in the world. As overcomers, Christians are not to suffer under many of the things we have accepted as normal.

KEYS TO THE KINGDOM - Instruction on how to gain authority in God's Kingdom through prayer is the topic of this book. Many principles and methods of prayer are covered, such as praying in the Spirit, fasting and prayer, travailing prayer, praise, intercession and spiritual warfare.

EXPOSING SATAN'S DEVICES - This book is a powerful expose' of Satan's tricks, tactics and lies. Cult and Occultic methods and groups are listed so Christians can detect their activity. Demon activity is discussed and deliverance and casting out demons is dealt with in detail. Satan's kingdom is uncovered and the Christian is taught to overcome through spiritual discernment and warfare.

HEALING OF THE SPIRIT, SOUL AND BODY - This book teaches how to overcome emotional problems, as well as physical ones, and how to receive divine healing. It also teaches how to renew the carnal mind and walk in the spirit of life, thereby overcoming depression, loneliness and fear.

NEITHER MALE NOR FEMALE - What is the woman's role in the church and home? Who is a woman's spiritual head and covering? Does God call women to the five-fold ministry? What does God's Word say about divorce, celibacy and choosing a marriage partner? These and other woman related topics are Scripturally examined.

EXTREMES OR BALANCE? - Many Christians have hurt the cause of Christ through "out-of-balance" teachings and demonstrations. This book shows how to avoid those areas. It also deals wisely with the excesses and extremes in the body of Christ.

THE PATHWAY INTO THE OVERCOMER'S WALK - This book contains answers to the questions an overcomer faces as he presses toward the prize of the high calling in Christ Jesus. How can we be conformed to the image of Christ? How does the Holy Spirit work with the overcomers in the end times? What are the overcomer's rewards?

PERSONAL SPIRITUAL WARFARE - Explains the invisible world of spiritual forces that influence our lives and how good can prevail over the evil around us as we prepare for the new kingdom age that is coming. This book will help you overcome problems in your finances, marriage, the emotional pressures of fear, anger and hurt. Here are the keys to victory through spiritual warfare.

MARK OF GOD OR MARK OF THE BEAST - Much has been written and said about the mark of the beast, but little has been said about the mark of God. What does the 666 mean and what is this mysterious mark? How is it linked to the world of finance? Has this mark already begun? This book answers many questions about the mark of the beast and the mark of God, and how they affect Christians.

Please visit our website for information on how to order the complete Overcoming Life Bible Study Series.

www.BibleResources.org

Purpose and Vision

> Go ye therefore, and teach all nations, baptizing them in the name of the Father, and of the Son, and of the Holy Ghost: Teaching them to observe all things whatsoever I have commanded you: and, lo, I am with you alway, even unto the end of the world. Amen.
>
> **Matthew 28:19,20**

Christ Unlimited is not "another denomination," sect, or just a separate group. It is an arm of the Body of Christ -- the Church of Jesus Christ, which has been called to strengthen the Body at large. We also believe we have been called to help establish the Kingdom of God in the earth.

Christ Unlimited is involved with all Bible-believing Christians regardless of their church or denominational affiliations and committed to helping wherever possible in evangelistic and teaching outreaches.

Christ Unlimited believes that time is running out and the Gospel has not been preached to every creature. Many nations have not heard the Gospel, and in many places, doors for evangelism are closing. We believe it is time all Christians cooperated with the Lord in breaking down denominational walls for a united front line against the kingdom of darkness and in setting up the Kingdom of the Lord Jesus Christ by the power of the Holy Spirit.

Christ Unlimited provides such tools as to enable the saints of God to establish the Kingdom of God in the earth. We encourage groups of prayer warriors who will pray, fast, and intercede for the nations. This, we believe, is weapon number one. We teach believers how to overcome through spiritual warfare and through knowing how to use their authority in Christ Jesus through the Word and the power of the Holy Spirit.

Christians need to know how to bring down the forces of darkness in their own lives and in the lives of those to whom they minister. We provide such tools as Bibles, literature, Christ Unlimited books and an online prayer ministry. We publish the Gospel going out via any means of communication; including the internet, videos, as well as literature. We have teaching seminars, Bible schools, and correspondence courses, all aimed at winning souls to Christ and building the Body of Christ into maturity.

Bud and Betty Miller serve the Lord together as founders of the multi-visioned ministry outreach, Christ Unlimited. The outreaches of this ministry have stemmed from a tremendous desire to see the Word of God taught in its balanced entirety. The Millers are firm believers in prayer and, through prayer, have seen many released from the bondages of fear, failure, and defeat.

The outreaches of Christ Unlimited are in obedience to the words of our Lord in **Mark 16:15**: **Go ye into all the world and preach the gospel to every creature.** This mandate from the Lord presents a challenge to our generation as an estimated 25 percent of the world's population still have not heard the Good News of Jesus Christ.

Christ Unlimited Ministries also is dedicated to teaching God's Word. **Hosea 4:6** says: **My people are destroyed for lack of knowledge.** Many Christians are leading defeated lives simply because they do not know God's Word in its fullest.

Christ Unlimited Ministries has provided for those who desire to know God's Word in a greater way. The main thrust of the teaching and literature is directed at "How to be an overcomer." In the endtimes, we must be prepared to overcome the onslaughts of Satan. Many Christians are suffering needlessly, because they do not know how to overcome sickness, depression, divorce, fear, and financial failure. Christ Unlimited Ministries provides answers for troubled families as well as trains workers for service.

44

www.ingramcontent.com/pod-product-compliance
Lightning Source LLC
Chambersburg PA
CBHW020344130626
46549CB00003B/1275